Conquista!

CONQUISTA!

Clyde Robert Bulla & *Michael Syson*

Illustrated by Ronald Himler

THOMAS Y. CROWELL · *New York*

Published simultaneously in Canada by Fitzhenry & Whiteside Limited,
Toronto. For information address Thomas Y. Crowell,
10 East 53rd Street, New York, N.Y. 10022. Designed by Harriett Barton
Manufactured in the United States of America

LIBRARY OF CONGRESS CATALOGING IN PUBLICATION DATA

Bulla, Clyde Robert. Conquista!
SUMMARY: At the time of Coronado's exploration
for a fabled city of gold, a young Indian boy
encounters his first horse.
* [1. Indians of North America—Fiction.*
2. America—Discovery and exploration—Fiction.
3. Horses—Fiction] I. Syson, Michael, joint
author. II. Himler, Ronald. III. Title.
PZ7.B912Co [Fic] 77-26585
ISBN 0-690-03870-4 0-690-03871-2 lib. bdg.

First Edition

To Joanna

Preface

*When Columbus reached America in 1492, an era of
exploration and conquest began. Not until later
were there many colonists who turned to farming,
mining, trade, and the building of cities. Most early
explorers set out for the New World to find sudden
wealth.*

*By 1521, the Spanish conqueror Cortés had taken
the gold-rich Aztec empire in Mexico. From there,
the Spaniards moved north and south. Indian armies
could not stand against them. The Spanish soldiers*

had superior weapons—crossbows, steel-bladed swords, and firearms. They had horses, as well.

In South America, Pizarro plundered the Incas and sent their gold to Spain. Other Spaniards traveled far into North America in search of treasure. One was Coronado. Much is known of his expedition, but there is much that can never be known. What follows is not a historical account. It tells what might have happened.

Conquista!

I

The man looked back at the troop of horsemen. They were *his* men; he was their leader. They must not know of his weariness and doubt. He sat straighter in the saddle and pushed on through the grassland— the ocean of green—that stretched ahead.

He was Don Francisco Vásquez de Coronado. In that year, 1541, he and his band had come north from Mexico in search of Quivira, fabled city of gold. It was a dream that haunted him now, hollowing his eyes and quickening his blood. Quivira and its gold for the

glory of Spain, for the glory of Coronado and those
of the name who would come after him!

He had led his men through mountains and desert.
They had made way for great herds of buffalo. They
had seen a few Indians who vanished as the Spaniards
drew near.

It was the horses the Indians feared, thought
Coronado. The horses from Spain that were still so
strange to the eyes of the savages. Indians in the south
had fled in terror at the sight of mounted men. They
had believed horse and rider were one: a fearful creature
from another world come to attack and destroy.

If he might question these savages—if he might
capture one who could show him the way . . .

What an empty land it was, not like the lands to the
south with their splendid cities and golden treasure. In
all this emptiness, could there truly be a city of gold?

Again he looked back at the troop and was cheered.
They made a brave show, the riders with their dancing
plumes and gleaming helmets. And the horses—
Arab, bay, chestnut, roan. . . .

With his horses he would find Quivira! He knew the
value of these wonderful beasts. In this wasteland a

horse could mean the difference between life and death.

He had warned his men, "Not one animal must escape." He had promised death to anyone who should lose his horse.

From time to time he had made a quick count to be sure that all were there. He counted them now—those that carried riders, then the extra horses that were being led.

His eyes blurred a little. Surely he was mistaken. Again he counted.

He saw the faces of the men near him. They were watching. They *knew*, he told himself, and dared not tell him.

One of the horses was missing.

II

The young man stood alone in the desert. He was slim and straight; his skin was deeply brown. He wore buckskin breeches, moccasins, and a necklace of seeds. With arms held high, he waited for his god.

A cool dawn wind touched his cheek. The sky glowed. Soon now—very soon—his god would rise out of the east in a blaze of crimson and gold.

His lips moved as he prayed: "Tell me what I seek to know. Send the vision that will let me know my man-name."

Too long he had borne the name his mother had given him. On the day of his birth, someone had brought a wolf cub to the village. For no other reason, his mother had called him Little Wolf.

As a child-name it had served well enough, but it was no name for him now.

Three times he had gone to the shaman, the medicine man of the tribe. Three times he had asked, "Where shall I find my man-name? Set a time for my journey and tell me where to go. Give me a sign."

The old shaman had taken Little Wolf's gifts— the food, the clothing, the necklaces. He had taken all and told the young man nothing.

Little Wolf had seen others go to the shaman's lodge. He had watched them leave on their journeys. He had seen them return with a firm step, as if they knew their future, as if they were sure of their manhood, and they were no older or braver than he.

Then, on Little Wolf's fourth visit, the shaman had spoken: "Follow the grey goose south to the great plain beyond the mountains, farther than any of our people have been before, until you meet the sun-god face to face."

"And what then?" the young man had asked.

But the shaman had not answered.

Little Wolf had made the journey. Now, in this land of scattered rocks and strange desert plants, he waited.

Even the wind seemed to wait. The colors in the sky grew deeper, brighter. The sun-god rose over the hills.

Little Wolf prayed: "Tell me what I seek to know. Give me a sign—"

A sound came to him, faint at first, then louder. It was like the beating of his own heart.

Thud, thud, thud.

He peered into the sun. The sound seemed to come from there. He shielded his eyes with his fingers. Out of the fiery brightness came a rising, falling shape.

An animal shape.

There were legs. There was a crooked hump. From the hump, something gleamed like the sun itself.

Little Wolf sank to the ground. The sun-god was angry. It had sent this devil to destroy him!

He closed his eyes.

8

The thud of footsteps came nearer. Then there was stillness.

Slowly he opened his eyes. The creature was there, looking down at him. It had four legs, a head, a long, thick tail, and on its back that crooked hump. It wore a headdress—or was it a part of the animal?—that looked as if leather thongs were fitted to its head and looped over its neck.

Like a big, grey elk or a great dog, it stood and watched him. Its eyes were round and bright.

It shook its head and made a jangling sound. The brush of hair on its neck lifted and fell. Its lips pulled back from its teeth, and it laughed—shrill, devilish laughter that turned Little Wolf cold with fear.

He tore open the leather pouch he wore on his belt. He thrust his hand inside it and drew out a dried hawk's wing, a few bones, and a handful of pebbles with sacred symbols. He threw them on the ground in front of him. Never taking his eyes from the animal, he drew a circle around himself with his forefinger.

Yet he knew the magic was not strong enough to save him. The animal—the sun devil—took a step nearer.

With one hand Little Wolf reached for the bow
slung on his back. With the other he reached into his
quiver for an arrow. There was one left. He fitted
it to his bowstring. He took aim at the animal's chest.
Its heart must be there—if it had a heart.

The sun was in his eyes. His hand shook as he
let fly.

He had missed!

But no—the arrow had struck home. He could see
the shaft of it deep in the crooked hump on the sun
devil's back.

And the animal did not fall. It did not cry out in
pain. It seemed to feel nothing.

Little Wolf sprang to his feet and fled.

III

The horse felt the cool earth beneath his feet. The growing things on the desert floor were damp with dew. He stopped to nibble at a patch of blue flowers.

The bridle reins had slipped high on his neck. The dangling stirrup struck his hind leg as he walked. On his first night alone, when he had tried to lie down, the saddle had twisted to one side. And there it hung, with a helmet, a sword, and a wine bottle tied to the pommel.

It was days since he and his rider had become

separated. The man had ridden up a small canyon and
dismounted to drink from a spring. Something like
a large cat had leaped across the rocks overhead,
and the horse had run away.

Afterward, recovered from his fright, he had waited.
Then he had moved on, seeking another who would claim
him.

But in all his wandering, he had found only this
odd man-creature who crouched before him, then ran
away.

IV

Little Wolf had not gone far. Ashamed of his fear, he had stopped. No more would he run. Here he would make a stand.

The grey devil again came toward him. Its head was a little like that of a deer, but longer. There was pride in the arch of its neck. There was strength in the shoulders and hind quarters.

It moved easily. Only the hump looked awkward, with the strange shapes that clung to it. His arrow was sticking out from among them.

Little Wolf was ready, knife in hand.

The creature came closer. Little Wolf stepped aside. He flung himself forward in a long leap that carried him up behind the hump. If he moved quickly, he might finish the work of the arrow. He struck with the knife. The blade bit deep.

He heard a dull crack. He was falling. He was on the ground, his legs gripping the animal's hump.

Again and again he stabbed with his knife. He twisted the blade, but no blood flowed.

He looked up. The animal stood nearby, watching him. . . .

Once Little Wolf had caught a lizard. It had darted away, leaving part of its tail in his hand. Had this creature tricked him in the same way? Had it shed its hump to save itself? Did the hump have a life of its own?

He ripped it with his knife. He picked it up, held it high, and flung it to the ground. A piece of metal that hung from it swung out and struck him on the head.

Little Wolf was stunned. He almost fell. He turned to face the creature. He was sure it was mocking him.

He looked down at the hump. Whatever it was, it was dead. Perhaps it had never been alive.

With his foot he prodded the thing at his feet. Tied to it was a sort of polished bowl. He pulled the bowl free and sniffed it. He could smell the scent of man.

Fastened to the bowl was a long, red plume. He tore it off and threw the bowl away. The plume he would take to show his people. No bird he knew wore feathers such as this.

Something else was tied to the hump—a long, slim knife that had slipped halfway out of its leather case. He threw the case aside. He held the blade by the handle and began to slash the air back and forth.

The animal flung up its head and danced backward.

Little Wolf whirled with the blade in both hands. He liked the whistling sound it made. He lifted it high over his head and brought it down on the hump. The long blade snapped in two. He tried to fit the pieces together, then let them fall.

There was something else fastened to the hump. It was round and blue, shaped like a gourd bottle. He pulled it free. Something gurgled inside.

He shook it. The top of the bottle exploded in a shower of pink foam that splashed his face.

He licked his lips. He tasted the liquid in the bottle.

It was strange—both sour and sweet—and it was sharp on his tongue.

He tasted it again. The drink warmed him; it was magic. He could feel its strength in his veins.

A thought came to him. This drink and the long knife were gifts of the sun-god.

He looked at the big, grey animal. Without its ugly hump, it was beautiful. It had not harmed him. Was this creature, too, a gift of the sun-god—his to take proudly back to the village?

While he watched, the creature bowed its head and bent its knees. It was lying down, rolling on its back. The big dog was playing!

Little Wolf laughed in sudden delight. He lay down, too. He rolled on *his* back, waving his legs in the air as the big dog had done.

But he was playing alone. The creature was on its feet, watching him with a puzzled look in its eyes.

Little Wolf felt foolish. He got up.

The creature was moving away, and the young man moved beside it.

The creature broke into a trot, then a lope. It left Little Wolf behind.

He did not stop. His pace was slower, but it was steady. The big dog had been sent to him. He must not lose it.

The creature was leading him on, waiting a few moments, then dashing off again. It started up a trail that led into the hills.

Little Wolf knew the trail. He had taken it yesterday. At one point it was narrow, with a rock wall on either side and a rock ledge above.

Running swiftly, he took a short cut to the ledge. If the animal came this far, he could surprise it. He might bring it to its knees and conquer it.

The thudding steps came near. The creature was passing beneath him. Little Wolf dropped off the ledge and onto its back.

The animal gave a kind of scream. It slipped in the loose rock and fell sideways to the ground. Little Wolf was thrown clear. The animal struggled to its feet, leaped over a line of boulders, and disappeared.

Little Wolf followed it. He found it nearby, tearing at a clump of grass with its teeth.

He gazed in wonder. Never before had he seen a dog eat grass.

He searched the desert floor. He found some stiff, coarse grass and held it out to the big dog.

The animal looked interested. It took a few steps forward.

Little Wolf waited. His eyes were on the headdress the creature wore—the headdress made of leather thongs. Part of it lay over the animal's neck and was fastened to something the animal held in its mouth.

The big dog stretched out its neck. Its teeth closed on the handful of grass.

Little Wolf gave a lunge. He seized the leather thong near the animal's mouth.

The animal plunged and reared. Little Wolf was lifted off his feet and flung from side to side.

The big dog stopped, legs braced, ears back. There was blood on its mouth.

If it lunged again, Little Wolf could not keep his hold on the thong. He knew it. He thought the animal knew it, too. One more lunge, and it would be free.

But if he were on the big dog's back— If he could wear down its strength and force it to its knees—

He let go of the thong. In the same motion he

grasped the thick hair on the creature's neck. His body twisted. He swung his leg up, and he was on the animal's back.

The animal was running. Little Wolf could hear the pounding hoofs beneath him as he bent forward.

He gripped the animal's sides with his legs. Slowly he raised himself until he was sitting upright.

The desert was flying past him—the earth, the rocks, the growing things. Once this land had made him feel small, but no longer. From here to the distant mountains would hardly be half a day's journey!

On the back of the sun dog he could race the wind. He could race an eagle and leave it far behind.

Never before had he known such power. He shouted, and his voice was strong above the thunder of hoofbeats. He lifted one hand and waved to the birds, to the mountains, to the sun.

He lifted the other hand and leaned into the wind. Then he was falling. He saw the earth rushing toward him. He struck the desert floor and lay still.

V

His eyes opened. He felt bruised and numb, but he
was smiling. His heart still beat with the wild joy he
had felt when he was on the creature's back, flying
between earth and sky.

The world had grown quiet. He looked about him.
The big dog was gone.

He tried to get up and gasped at the stab of pain
in his leg. He fell back upon the ground.

He opened the top of his moccasin. Blood was seeping
from a cut in his ankle. He pulled up a tuft of grass

and packed it, roots and all, about the wound, then
drew the moccasin thong tight.

He stood up. The big dog's tracks were plain in the
loose earth. He walked in the trail. Dragging his foot
painfully, he kept on, stumbling, falling, rising again.

Toward the mountains. Into the foothills. He was
weak from loss of blood. He closed his mind to the pain.

The creature's trail was still clear, but night was
near. In the morning the sun dog might be gone forever.

He climbed up into a box canyon. On three sides
it was closed in by high cliffs.

The sun dog was there, standing still, its head
lifted.

They faced each other, and suddenly he was
stricken with shame. This great animal had come
from the sun-god, and he had fought it as he might
have fought an enemy. He had wounded it, made it
suffer. Now he was wounded and suffering in return.

The big grey dog looked as if it were waiting for
something. But what? What was left for him to do?

He could only go.

He turned and walked away.

The canyon was deep in shadow. Beyond was the sunset. He wanted to say to his god, "I was proud and vain, like a child. I was not ready. Give me a sign that you hear me, that I may be forgiven," but now he was shamed. He was humbled. He could not speak the words.

He limped on. A sound came from behind him—a familiar footstep. He began to tremble. The sun dog was following him!

It came so near that he could feel its breath on his shoulder. He could have reached up and taken hold of the thong that lay on its neck, but he made no move toward it.

They walked together out of the canyon. The sunset cast arrows of light high into the sky. He prayed aloud, "Let this day be with me always. Let my man-name be He Who Rides the Sun Dog." And it seemed to him that the sun-god smiled.

VI

One more day, then another and another, and
Coronado's last hope died. In all this cruel, empty land
there was no city of gold. He was sure of it now.
Broken and defeated, he led his men back the way
they had come.

But for the Indians of North America a new era
had begun. The sun dog remained, and over the years
others appeared. Under the Indians' care, they
multiplied. On horseback, whole nations moved out
of the barren mountains and into the fertile plains.

On horseback, Indians could follow the buffalo herds that provided them with most of their needs. Thus they came to a golden age that was to last three hundred years.

About the Book

The book *Conquista!* grew out of a chance conversation several years ago in which Michael Syson was describing to Clyde Robert Bulla a short film he had recently written, produced, and directed. Mr. Bulla became fascinated by the story, which in the film is told essentially without words. Mr. Syson and he both felt it could be equally effective—though in an altogether different way—in book form, and working in close collaboration, they set out to adapt the story for young readers. The film version of *Conquista!* has appeared in motion-picture theaters and on television throughout Europe, the United States, and Canada, as well as in many other parts of the world.

About the Authors

Clyde Robert Bulla is one of America's best-known and most-beloved writers of books for children. The author of more than fifty distinguished books, including *The Beast of Lor*, *Pocahontas and the Strangers*, and *Shoeshine Girl*, he has been widely praised for his rare ability to write simply yet with unusual warmth and sensitivity about the concerns of young people. Mr. Bulla loves to travel when he is not busy writing at his home in Los Angeles.

Michael Syson is an English writer and film-maker who has long been interested in early American history. A lieutenant in the British navy in World War II, he has since worked extensively in radio and television in both New York and London. Mr. Syson lives in London's Chelsea and does much of his writing in a country cottage in Sussex.

About the Illustrator

Ronald Himler was born in Cleveland Ohio, and studied at the Cleveland Institute of Art. He has illustrated a number of books for children, and is both author and illustrator of the picture book, *Girl on the Yellow Giraffe*. Mr. Himler lives with his wife and their three children in New York City.